Let's Get Moving™

The MARCHING Book

Maya Glass

The Rosen Publishing Group's
PowerStart Press™
New York

1

Published in 2004 by The Rosen Publishing Group, Inc.
29 East 21st Street, New York, NY 10010

First Edition

Book Design: Maria E. Melendez
Developmental Editor: Nancy Allison, Certified Movement Analyst, Registered Movement Educator

Photo Credits: All photos by Maura B. McConnell except p. 21 by Nancy Opitz.

Library of Congress Cataloging-in-Publication Data

Glass, Maya.
The marching book / by Maya Glass.— 1st ed.
     p. cm. — (Let's get moving)
Includes index.
Summary: Pictures and brief captions describe the movements involved in marching.
  ISBN 1-4042-2516-1
1. Marching drills—Juvenile literature. [1. Marching drills.] I. Title. II. Series.
  GV1797 .G53 2004
  791—dc21
                                                              2003008017

Manufactured in the United States of America

Contents

I march.

5

I march forward.

I march backward.

9

I march in a circle.

11

I march in
a line.

13

I swing my arms
when I march.

15

I march with very
small steps.

17

I march with very
big steps.

19

I march and march and march.

Marching is fun!

23

Words to Know

backward

forward

step

swing

Index

Web Sites

Due to the changing nature of Internet links, PowerStart Press has developed an online list of Web sites related to the subject of this book. This site is updated regularly. Please use this link to access the list:
www.powerkidslinks.com/lgmov/march/

24